The Lovey that Came to Life

Written by Karen M. Bobos
Illustrated by Emily Hercock

Please visit BobosBabes.com

Published by Bobos Babes, Ltd.

ISBN: 978-1-7374375-8-1 Hardback Edition

ISBN: 978-1-7374375-9-8 Paperback Edition

United States

Dedication

I still remember the day when I saw this plush bear on the store shelf.
He was adorable and sweet, and well . . . I just couldn't help myself.

I rubbed my pregnant belly and said, "I think I found you a friend."
I awaited the day for her to meet him to play make believe and pretend.

For years, my Scarlett and her Pete have been at each other's side.
A life filled with giggles and dancing – oh, such a joyful ride.

Never could I have imagined how loved this sweet bear would be.
This book is dedicated to the innocent love that a child finds in her lovey.

In a world where creatures co-exist
And love is the common theme,
There were three little sisters,
Living the life of every little girl's dream.

Angel Scarlett, Princess Daphne, and Fairy Cora
Were the sisters' names.
Each sister had her own special talent;
Some would call them magical dames.

Angel Scarlett was the oldest sister.
She had exquisiteness and a heart of gold.
She had heavenly skin with magical powers
And a kind and gentle soul.

Princess Daphne was the middle sister,
A spitfire beauty full of life and fun.
She loved adventure and glam
And had the vision to see the good in everyone.

Fairy Cora was the littlest sister.
She had the sweetest spirit and warmest smile,
A wise babe with the ability to hear
The softest sounds from far beyond a mile.

The sisters were called "The Bobos Babes"
By all of the creatures in Harmony,
A land where most can escape to
Only in their mind to feel ultimately free.

They lived in a castle behind an enchanted waterfall
With warm shimmery mist
That fell into a glistening stream
Where the hummingbirds fly and pink fish kiss.

Although Angel Scarlett was as close
To her two sisters as could be,
She also had a very special confidant,
Her Polar Bear Pete, her lovey.

Polar Bear Pete, a stuffed animal,
Was Angel Scarlett's very first friend.
They loved playing games
And using their imagination to pretend.

Pete wasn't like other lovies;
He was much more than a toy.
He provided Angel Scarlett
Friendship, comfort, love, and joy.

One day when Angel Scarlett
Was hugging Pete with all of her might,
She accidentally used her heavenly powers
To bring her stuffed animal to life.

All it took was a warm embrace
And a sweet angel kiss,
And Pete's heart started beating
As he shared a smile of bliss.

Pete snuggled and cuddled
With Angel Scarlett every night.
During the day, he played in a special area
Of the castle called Arctic Delight.

Angel Scarlett created Arctic Delight
With her heavenly powers
To keep her polar bear lovey
Cool for hours upon hours.

Pete loved swimming in the cool waters
And catching fish to eat.
He loved playing in the snow
And floating on ice blocks for a special treat.

Sometimes Angel Scarlett would play
With Polar Bear Pete all day,
Making snow angels and snow bears
To pass the time away.

One morning, Angel Scarlett woke up
To find that Pete was not in her bed.
She looked behind her pillows,
Under her blankets, and beneath her bedspread.

She whistled for him
And called him by name.
She wondered if perhaps
He was playing a game.

"Come out. Come out, wherever you are!"
She shouted for Polar Bear Pete.
But he did not answer,
And Angel Scarlett was beginning to feel defeat.

"What's wrong, Angel Scarlett?"
Fairy Cora said, waking with a yawn.
"Pete's missing!" Angel Scarlett said, sobbing uncontrollably.
"He is just gone!"

"What do you mean?" said Princess Daphne,
Still waking from her sleep.
"I woke up," said Scarlett, "and looked everywhere,
But I cannot find my Pete!"

"Don't worry, Angel Scarlett," said Fairy Cora,
"He could not have gone far.
Did you try using your powers to find him?
Have you tried wishing on a star?"

"He never leaves before I awake,
Always making sure that my day starts off right."
Scarlett continued, "We planned on spending today
Flying our brand-new kite."

"Perhaps that is where he is," Princess Daphne said,
"Prepping for your day of fun.
Let's go to the hills where the best winds are
To see if that is what he has done."

The Bobos Babes hopped on their giant dog, Luke,
And headed for the hills
Where the breezes were so strong,
They were lined with purple windmills.

"He's not here!" cried Angel Scarlett.
"He is nowhere to be found.
We've searched the hills, examined the trees,
And even combed the ground."

"We need to check Arctic Delight!"
Shouted Fairy Cora. "Of course, he is there.
We should have thought of there
When we began looking for your polar bear."

The Babes hurried back to the castle
And headed straight to Arctic Delight,
Hoping their cold weather-loving friend
Was enjoying a glacial breakfast bite.

But he wasn't. Pete was not in Arctic Delight
Where they had hoped he would be.
Angel Scarlett was beyond worried,
As his whereabouts were a complete mystery.

"He's never left me before," said Scarlett.
"We always start the day with a laugh.
Then we end the day wishing on stars
After each taking our bubble bath."

"Please don't cry, dear sister," said Fairy Cora.
"I am sure Pete is fine.
He will be back before you know it;
I am sure he just lost track of time."

The sisters quietly walked back to their quarters,
Trying to keep their spirits high.
They couldn't help but wonder
What happened to the sweet arctic lovey guy.

"Let's head to the highest tower for breakfast.
Some food will help us think,"
Said Princess Daphne. "Food will give us
The brain power to find the missing link."

When the girls reached the tower
And entered their indoor dining room,
To their surprise, it was adorned
With yellow daffodils and every color balloon.

The table was filled from each end
With every possible delicious breakfast dish,
From cinnamon rolls to exotic fruit trays
To lox platters with smoked salmon fish.

"Yum!" said Angel Scarlett.
"These are all of my favorite foods to eat.
Who created this amazing breakfast for us?
What a special treat!"

"Surprise!" said a little voice
Coming from the kitchen chamber way.
The girls looked to see who it was,
And their worries melted away.

Polar Bear Pete was holding a plate
Of warm homemade donuts with icing on top.
"What took you so long, Bobos Babes?
I was nervous my soufflé would flop."

"Pete!" The Babes ran to their friend
And showered him with hugs and love.
"We searched all morning for you
In every spot that we could think of."

"I'm so sorry, Babes!" Pete said.
"I didn't mean to make you worry.
I wanted to surprise you with this breakfast
And thought I'd be back in a hurry."

"Breakfast?" asked Fairy Cora,
"Oh Pete, this is an amazing feast!
Is that a strawberry rhubarb pie?" She exclaimed,
"Oh, I must have a piece!"

"Pete, when did you learn to cook
And bake and create such an amazing spread?"
Princess Daphne looked at the food in awe.
"Yum! Chocolate-chip banana bread!"

"I've been taking lessons from David the Dragonfly.
He's the best chef in the land.
My intention was to surprise you.
I'm sorry I scared you. I hope you understand.

Angel Scarlett," Pete continued, "you gave me life.
Please know this much is true.
I love you. I would never leave you.
Now sit and enjoy my cheese fondue!"

The Babes and the bear enjoyed their breakfast
From every muffin to every tart,
Cherishing their friendship
And never worrying again about being apart.

CPSIA information can be obtained
at www.ICGtesting.com
Printed in the USA
LVHW072110220122
708378LV00019BC/524

The Lovey that Came to Life

Written by Karen M. Bobos
Illustrated by Emily Hercock

Please visit BobosBabes.com

Published by Bobos Babes, Ltd.

ISBN: 978-1-7374375-8-1 Hardback Edition

ISBN: 978-1-7374375-9-8 Paperback Edition

United States

Dedication

I still remember the day when I saw this plush bear on the store shelf.
He was adorable and sweet, and well . . . I just couldn't help myself.

I rubbed my pregnant belly and said, "I think I found you a friend."
I awaited the day for her to meet him to play make believe and pretend.

For years, my Scarlett and her Pete have been at each other's side.
A life filled with giggles and dancing – oh, such a joyful ride.

Never could I have imagined how loved this sweet bear would be.
This book is dedicated to the innocent love that a child finds in her lovey.

In a world where creatures co-exist
And love is the common theme,
There were three little sisters,
Living the life of every little girl's dream.

Angel Scarlett, Princess Daphne, and Fairy Cora
Were the sisters' names.
Each sister had her own special talent;
Some would call them magical dames.

Angel Scarlett was the oldest sister.
She had exquisiteness and a heart of gold.
She had heavenly skin with magical powers
And a kind and gentle soul.

Princess Daphne was the middle sister,
A spitfire beauty full of life and fun.
She loved adventure and glam
And had the vision to see the good in everyone.

Fairy Cora was the littlest sister.
She had the sweetest spirit and warmest smile,
A wise babe with the ability to hear
The softest sounds from far beyond a mile.

The sisters were called "The Bobos Babes"
By all of the creatures in Harmony,
A land where most can escape to
Only in their mind to feel ultimately free.

They lived in a castle behind an enchanted waterfall
With warm shimmery mist
That fell into a glistening stream
Where the hummingbirds fly and pink fish kiss.

Although Angel Scarlett was as close
To her two sisters as could be,
She also had a very special confidant,
Her Polar Bear Pete, her lovey.

Polar Bear Pete, a stuffed animal,
Was Angel Scarlett's very first friend.
They loved playing games
And using their imagination to pretend.

Pete wasn't like other lovies;
He was much more than a toy.
He provided Angel Scarlett
Friendship, comfort, love, and joy.

One day when Angel Scarlett
Was hugging Pete with all of her might,
She accidentally used her heavenly powers
To bring her stuffed animal to life.

All it took was a warm embrace
And a sweet angel kiss,
And Pete's heart started beating
As he shared a smile of bliss.

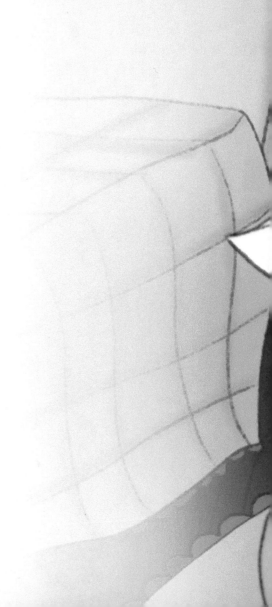

Pete snuggled and cuddled
With Angel Scarlett every night.
During the day, he played in a special area
Of the castle called Arctic Delight.

Angel Scarlett created Arctic Delight
With her heavenly powers
To keep her polar bear lovey
Cool for hours upon hours.

Pete loved swimming in the cool waters
And catching fish to eat.
He loved playing in the snow
And floating on ice blocks for a special treat.

Sometimes Angel Scarlett would play
With Polar Bear Pete all day,
Making snow angels and snow bears
To pass the time away.

One morning, Angel Scarlett woke up
To find that Pete was not in her bed.
She looked behind her pillows,
Under her blankets, and beneath her bedspread.

She whistled for him
And called him by name.
She wondered if perhaps
He was playing a game.

"Come out. Come out, wherever you are!"
She shouted for Polar Bear Pete.
But he did not answer,
And Angel Scarlett was beginning to feel defeat.

"What's wrong, Angel Scarlett?"
Fairy Cora said, waking with a yawn.
"Pete's missing!" Angel Scarlett said, sobbing uncontrollably.
"He is just gone!"

"What do you mean?" said Princess Daphne,
Still waking from her sleep.
"I woke up," said Scarlett, "and looked everywhere,
But I cannot find my Pete!"

"Don't worry, Angel Scarlett," said Fairy Cora,
"He could not have gone far.
Did you try using your powers to find him?
Have you tried wishing on a star?"

"He never leaves before I awake,
Always making sure that my day starts off right."
Scarlett continued, "We planned on spending today
Flying our brand-new kite."

"Perhaps that is where he is," Princess Daphne said,
"Prepping for your day of fun.
Let's go to the hills where the best winds are
To see if that is what he has done."

The Bobos Babes hopped on their giant dog, Luke,
And headed for the hills
Where the breezes were so strong,
They were lined with purple windmills.

"He's not here!" cried Angel Scarlett.
"He is nowhere to be found.
We've searched the hills, examined the trees,
And even combed the ground."

"We need to check Arctic Delight!"
Shouted Fairy Cora. "Of course, he is there.
We should have thought of there
When we began looking for your polar bear."

The Babes hurried back to the castle
And headed straight to Arctic Delight,
Hoping their cold weather-loving friend
Was enjoying a glacial breakfast bite.

But he wasn't. Pete was not in Arctic Delight
Where they had hoped he would be.
Angel Scarlett was beyond worried,
As his whereabouts were a complete mystery.

"He's never left me before," said Scarlett.
"We always start the day with a laugh.
 Then we end the day wishing on stars
After each taking our bubble bath."

"Please don't cry, dear sister," said Fairy Cora.
"I am sure Pete is fine.
He will be back before you know it;
I am sure he just lost track of time."

The sisters quietly walked back to their quarters,
Trying to keep their spirits high.
They couldn't help but wonder
What happened to the sweet arctic lovey guy.

"Let's head to the highest tower for breakfast.
Some food will help us think,"
Said Princess Daphne. "Food will give us
The brain power to find the missing link."

When the girls reached the tower
And entered their indoor dining room,
To their surprise, it was adorned
With yellow daffodils and every color balloon.

The table was filled from each end
With every possible delicious breakfast dish,
From cinnamon rolls to exotic fruit trays
To lox platters with smoked salmon fish.

"Yum!" said Angel Scarlett.
"These are all of my favorite foods to eat.
Who created this amazing breakfast for us?
What a special treat!"

"Surprise!" said a little voice
Coming from the kitchen chamber way.
The girls looked to see who it was,
And their worries melted away.

Polar Bear Pete was holding a plate
Of warm homemade donuts with icing on top.
"What took you so long, Bobos Babes?
I was nervous my soufflé would flop."

"Pete!" The Babes ran to their friend
And showered him with hugs and love.
"We searched all morning for you
In every spot that we could think of."

"I'm so sorry, Babes!" Pete said.
"I didn't mean to make you worry.
I wanted to surprise you with this breakfast
And thought I'd be back in a hurry."

"Breakfast?" asked Fairy Cora,
"Oh Pete, this is an amazing feast!
Is that a strawberry rhubarb pie?" She exclaimed,
"Oh, I must have a piece!"

"Pete, when did you learn to cook
And bake and create such an amazing spread?"
Princess Daphne looked at the food in awe.
"Yum! Chocolate-chip banana bread!"

"I've been taking lessons from David the Dragonfly.
He's the best chef in the land.
My intention was to surprise you.
I'm sorry I scared you. I hope you understand.

Angel Scarlett," Pete continued, "you gave me life.
Please know this much is true.
I love you. I would never leave you.
Now sit and enjoy my cheese fondue!"

The Babes and the bear enjoyed their breakfast
From every muffin to every tart,
Cherishing their friendship
And never worrying again about being apart.

CPSIA information can be obtained
at www.ICGtesting.com
Printed in the USA
LVHW072110220122
708378LV00019BC/524